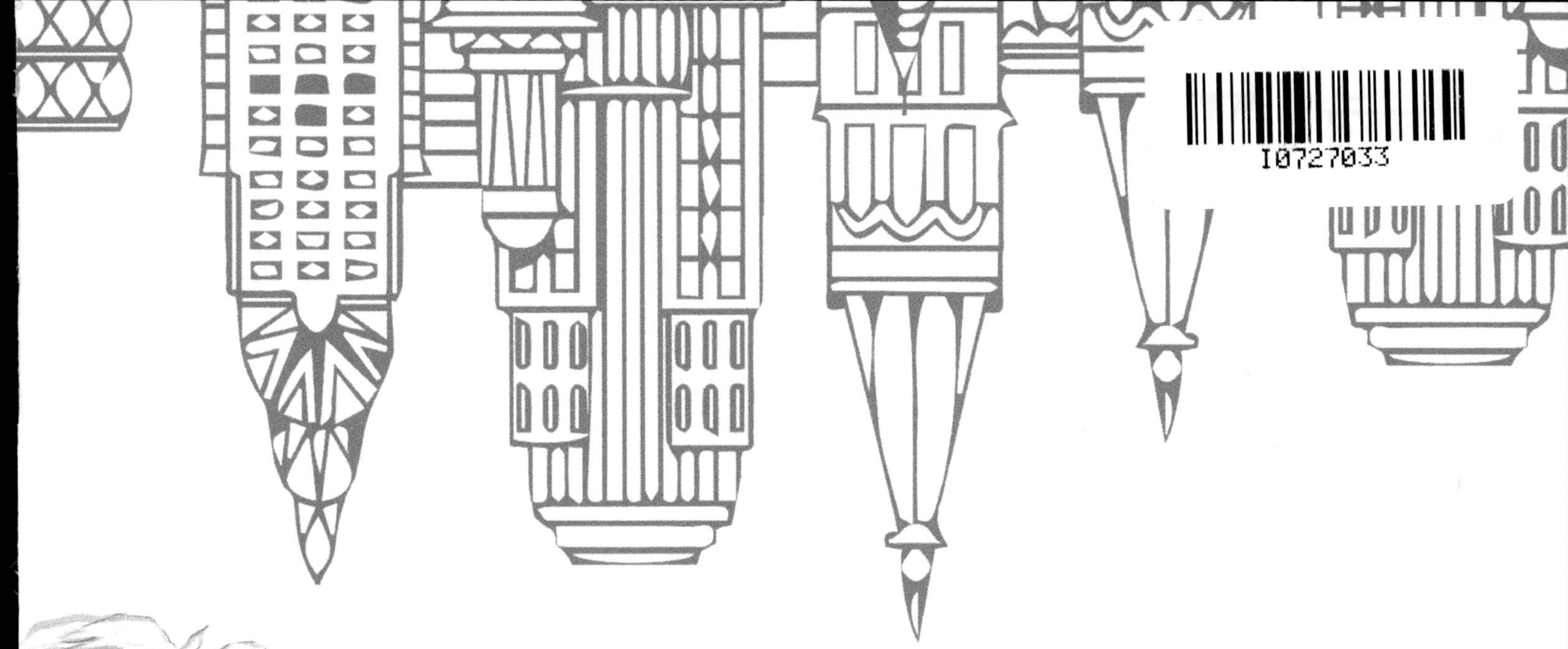

M.A. PHIPPS

PROJECT W. A. R.

THE OFFICIAL COLORING BOOK

ILLUSTRATED BY **ARNILD ALDEPOLLA**

PROJECT W.A.R.
SERIES COLORING BOOK

Copyright © 2022 M. A. Phipps
WWW.MAPHIPPS.COM
WWW.BOOKISHDEN.COM

Cover and Interior Artwork by Arnild Aldepolla
Interior Formatting by We Got You Covered Book Design
WWW.WEGOTYOUCOVEREDBOOKDESIGN.COM

SHIRE-HILL PUBLICATIONS
UNITED KINGDOM

ISBN: 978-1-914483-19-6

CONTENT WARNING

*This coloring book contains spoilers for all three books in the
Project W. A. R. trilogy as well as images some may find distressing.*

If you color these pictures and want to share them on social media, use
#COLORINGPROJECTWAR *so I can see your masterpieces!*

DON'T STAND OUT.

BLEND IN.

REMAIN INVISIBLE.

ULTRAXENOPIA

Chewing on the inside of my lower lip, I glance down to assess my desktop. The computerized screen is deactivated, and in the top left corner, a red light burns under the glass, flickering in and out like a flame. Swallowing, I hold my wrist out over the sensor, spurring the computer to life. White floods my field of vision apart from where my name is emblazoned in large black letters across the top of the screen.

WYNTER A. REEVES

Today's date appears underneath it: October 14th, 2061. A longer number is printed just below that, which reads 73956241. I'd know that number anywhere. Hell, I know it as well as I know my own name. It's my identification number. The number I was assigned at birth to designate my place in the State. In many ways, that number is all I am.

Other than that, the screen is blank.

The air is thick with dust, but through the impairing fog, I recognize my surroundings. I glimpse the familiar sight of the Heart in the details crumbling around me. But there are no people crowding the streets. No lights. No sign of life at all. There's only me, standing here all alone, as the world I once knew succumbs to destruction.

Panic boils beneath my skin, squeezing my lungs in a vise grip. My eyes close on instinct, but some unseen power wrenches them open again, forcing me to watch every second of this nightmare. To see what I can only assume must be the end of the world.

In the blink of an eye, the destruction explodes in a torrent of flame, devouring everything. A blinding flash burns across my vision, but when it clears, the desolate landscape is nowhere to be seen.

WYNTER A. REEVES

AGE: 18-20

BLOOD TYPE: O-

HEIGHT: 5'7

HAIR COLOR: BRUNETTE

EYE COLOR: MIXED; HETEROCHROMIA

[R: BLUE; L: GREEN]

WYNTER REEVES
WYNTER REEVES

"Since you had yet to be reassigned to a new sector at the time you were apprehended, you were still technically and lawfully under the guardianship of your mother. She has since relinquished her custodial rights, and you are now under the care and ownership of the State. Well…" He pauses. "The DSD, if we're being precise."

My eyes widen, and my blood runs cold. The DSD. The Department of Scientific Discoveries—a harmless enough name that ironically coincides with the last place in the world I would ever want to be. The DSD makes Detention look like a playground and is where the State conducts human experimentation, poorly hidden behind the guise of research. It's also the home of Termination. The home of everyone's worst nightmare. Only criminals and those determined to be unredeemable are sent here, so what could they possibly want with me? Am I a criminal?

Am I unredeemable?

"This is your home for the foreseeable future."

73956241
WYNTER A. REEVES

A buzzing sound fills my ears as a dew of sweat beads across my skin, a growl of frustration swelling in my throat as fear and anger go to war in my chest. Clenching my jaw, I peer sideways, watching Dr. Richter out of my peripheral vision. His back is turned toward me, his attention fixed on a glowing blue hologram screen above the white counter.

Beside him, a panel in the countertop opens, revealing a wide glass tube that looks to be at least a foot in diameter. It rises up, containing a handful of small silver objects, which float as if suspended in water. A purple aura pulsates around them as they orbit each other like tiny planets.

Dr. Richter nods. "Introduce the inhibitor."

Remembering the shard of mirror pressed close to my wrist, I shake the glass piece loose from my sleeve. The jagged edges dig into my palm. "Stay away from me," I whisper.

The woman inches toward me, disregarding my warnings, her hand clutching the syringe. My fingers tighten around the glass.

"I said stay away from me!" My arm shoots upward as I brandish the broken piece of mirror like a knife.

The woman hesitates, pausing mid-step, assessing the threat with a curious tilt of her head. I blink a few times to bring her face into focus, but her features are a blur, the sweat dripping into my eyes blinding me as I scramble for a way to escape this. But there is no escape, is there? The only way this ends is with me back on that table.

The only way this ends is with me dead.

EZRA J. LARAMIE

AGE: 22-24

BLOOD TYPE: A+

HEIGHT: 6'1

HAIR COLOR: BLOND

EYE COLOR: HAZEL

EZRA LARAMIE

My heart slams into my ribs as I pivot on my stool. When our eyes meet, he jerks his chin toward my glass, his gaze flashing briefly down and then back up again, locking on mine. I glance at the barely touched liquid, embarrassed.

He swings around on his own stool to face me. "You're not from around here." It's not a question.

"I'm here on business," I answer quickly.

"Business?" Skepticism creases his brow, a slight smile tugging up one corner of his mouth as he throws back the rest of his drink. "There isn't much business going down in Zone 7."

My throat tightens. "Not even with PHOENIX?"

The stool legs creak as he shifts over onto the seat between us, bringing himself closer to me. Leaning in so his lips are practically touching my ear, he growls, "I don't know who you are, but you won't find anything involved with PHOENIX here. I'd stop looking if I were you."

Vega

"Are you all right?" Her fingers are warm as she places a gentle hand on my arm.

I flinch away from her touch, giving a quick jerky nod, but my unsteady breaths reveal the truth I'm too much of a coward to voice. My lips quiver with the threat of a sob as I wipe the moisture from my face.

"I had a dream about my father. About the last time I saw him alive."

"I'm sorry," she whispers, her voice consoling.

I don't know how to react to her sentiment. In the Heart, we're encouraged not to show our grief, and above all, never to express it to others, especially if the person our grief is aimed at was found guilty of breaking the law. *"Enemies of the State don't deserve to be mourned."* That's what the State has always taught us. And yet, even now, years later, I still can't help mourning my father.

"You know," Jenner says, his voice dropping to a rumbling whisper, "Despite everything, I'm surprised Ezra let you come with us." His eyes turn back to mine, holding me to him, and my stomach clenches as the weight of my returning uncertainty bears down on my shoulders.

From the moment Ezra relented to my request, I've wondered about his unspoken motives. Why am I here? What help can I be to these people? Why did he let me come? Surely, he didn't only agree just because he knew I'd fight him on the matter.

"Why?" I ask past the sudden tightness in my throat.

Jenner shrugs. "Well, if the transmission really is a trap set by the DSD, we stand to lose the one thing that could give us the advantage against them."

RAINA M. DORNE

AGE: 24-26

BLOOD TYPE: AB+

HEIGHT: 5'9

HAIR COLOR: BRUNETTE

EYE COLOR: BROWN

RAI DORNE

My eyes brim with tears as my fingers stroke a handful of keys, pressing down just enough to call up each note. As the ping of the strings bounces off the tiled walls, echoing throughout the small space, I recall the melody my father once taught me. I wish I had thought to ask how he knew it.

His face springs to the forefront of my thoughts, and in my memory, I hear the gentle lilt of his voice instructing me to follow his hands. I strike each note at the same moment he does, playing side by side—my father in the past and me in the present—as if we're finally together again. As the music grows, the memory in my head changes.

Behind my closed eyelids, all I see is his face, bloodied and beaten rather than smiling—the way I wish I remembered him. The happy memories were tarnished the moment the State stepped into our lives, and now, instead of his warm voice guiding me, all I hear are the words that have tormented me for years.

"I'm sorry, Wynter."

Ezra smiles, as if he knows what I'm thinking, and flattens a hand against the small of my back, pulling me even closer. Then, as if gravity itself is pulling us together, he bends down at the same moment I rise onto my toes, meeting each other halfway.

Just like in my dream, Ezra's lips press to mine, and as the heat from my body melts into his, I stare at his closed eyes, trying to make sense of what's happening. My heart is pounding so furiously I struggle to inhale as it repeatedly slams into my ribs, and my frenzied nerves are pulling my senses in a thousand different directions at once. Pleasure and pain course through my veins, hand in hand.

When we break apart, the raging hurricane of my inexperienced emotions threatens to suffocate me. I gape at Ezra, afraid to blink or speak.

"I don't want you to go," he says, his voice soft. His words are warm against my face as he says them, each one a separate kiss of their own. The touch of them sends a shiver over my skin. "Stay here. Stay with me."

A PLACE FOR EVERYONE.

EVERYONE IN THEIR PLACE.

TYPE X

In this moment, Wynter Reeves doesn't exist. The weapon is in control of what happens now.

An outcry of chaos erupts through the plaza, and shouting intermingles with the clicking of metal as the soldiers all aim their weapons at me. When I step forward, the officer belts out another order, this time to the entire battalion. His squawking voice is followed by a torrent of gunfire.

My march forward is effortless as my mind redirects the rain of bullets with practiced ease. The shell casings fall around me in sheets, pinging off the cobblestone like discarded coins. I am a rock, and their attempts are like water, but still, the soldiers keep firing.

As the distance between us diminishes, the enemy's terror becomes palpable—a taste I savor on my tongue because this task demands it of me. Even the projectiles launched by the tanks fail to hit their target. With a flick of my wrist, the barrels bend back on themselves, preventing any further attempts.

I gape at the unknown Enforcer, but the chaos of the explosion has muddled my head and everything is happening too quickly for me to use my power to find out who he is or what he's hoping to accomplish. Why would an Enforcer attack his own unit?

Was this attack because of me?

He's so close to me now, every footstep a countdown to an end I'm no longer prepared for. My lips part to speak, but the thrashing wind rips the air from my lungs, the howling descent swallowing my voice.

Grunting, I glare into the black shield masking the Enforcer's face, wondering what he's waiting for. As if reading my mind, he raises his gun, and I tense, preparing myself for the shot, eager for the freedom it will grant me. An escape from this life.

He hesitates for only a second before muttering, "I promise, someday, you'll thank me for this."

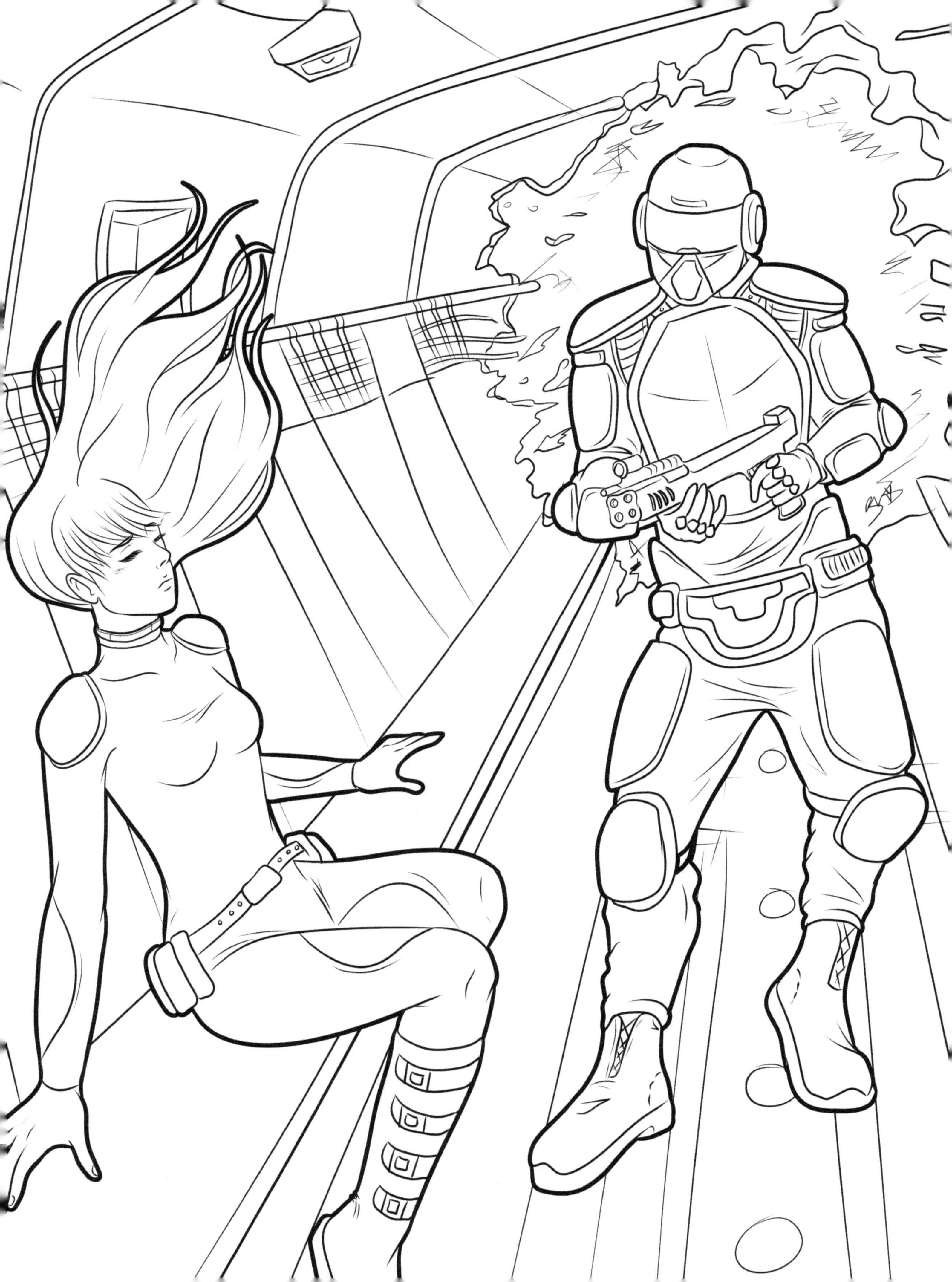

JENNER S. RHODES

AGE: 20-22

BLOOD TYPE: B-

HEIGHT: 6'3

HAIR COLOR: BLACK

EYE COLOR: BLUE

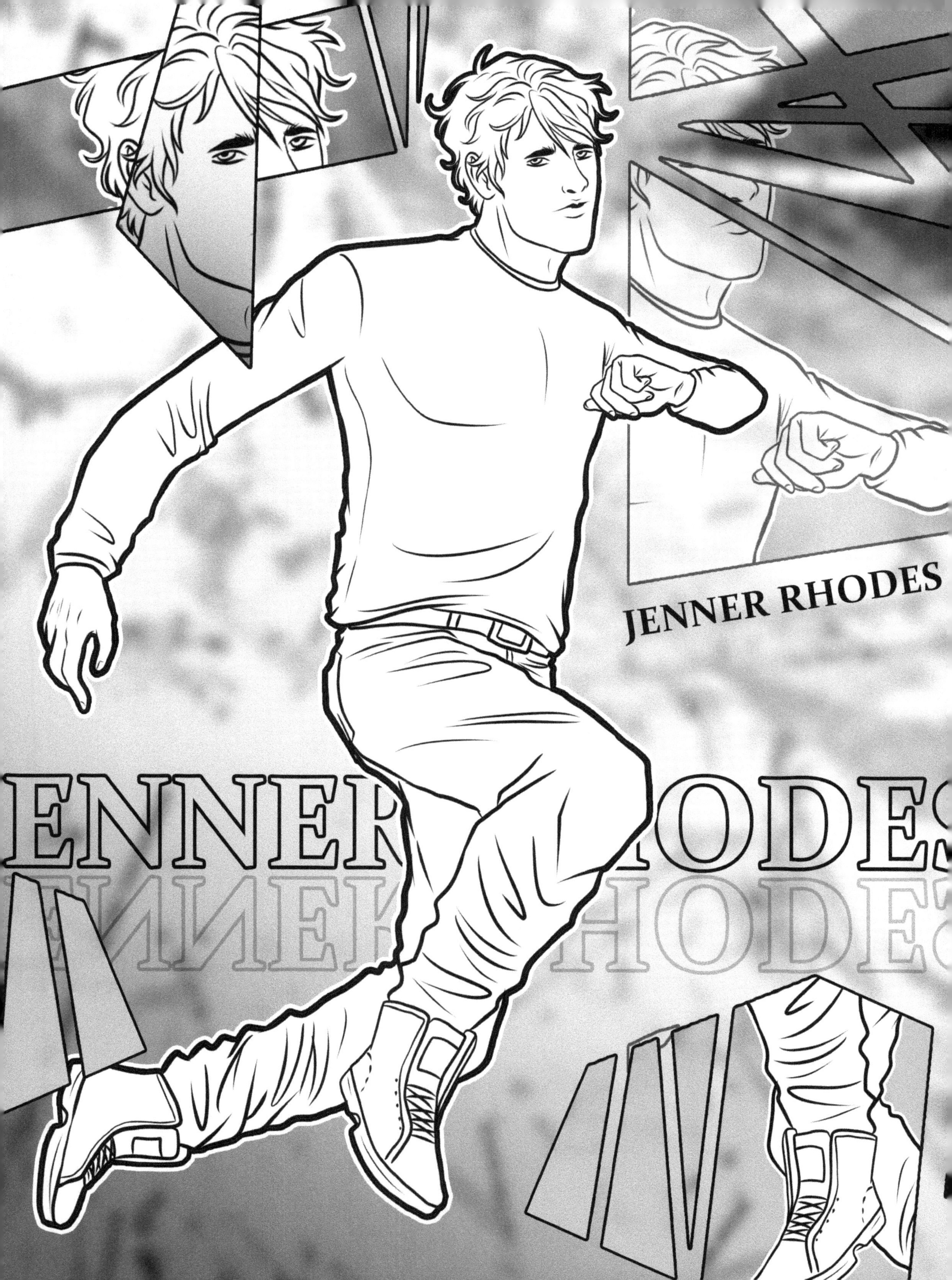

JENNER RHODES
JENNER
RODES

"Hello, Wynter. My name is Rodrick Nolan."

Based on the way he pauses now, I know this is the part of our conversation where I'm meant to introduce myself. Considering he already knows my name, I fail to see the point. I scowl instead.

He clears his throat. "We've met before. Roughly two and a half years ago now. Do you remember?"

I bite down on my tongue to keep my face blank, even though, on the inside, the madness always lingering at the edge of my sanity reaches out yet again. I don't remember this man, but I also don't remember much between my placement exam and when I returned to Dr. Richter's care. That missing chunk of time in my memory… If this man is telling the truth, then he might possess the answers as to what I'm forgetting. He might know why I gave myself up to the State.

He might know what I was so determined to protect.

A shrill beeping interrupts the thunderous hum as a beam of blue light shines through the torn curtains. Beside me, Ezra presses his hands to his ears to drown out the loud scream of the scanner, but I refuse to hinder my senses now that the drugs have finally worked their way out of my body. Pain drills into my back teeth as the high-pitched wail continues, the light touching every inch of the room except for the window's one blind spot—our hiding place. The beam finds even the darkest corners as it searches for any signs of life.

After a few minutes, the scan ends and the blue light dissolves as quickly as it spread. Gradually, the humming dies away and blissful silence returns, although my dread remains. Once the sound is out of earshot, Ezra and I flip onto our knees and risk a glance out the cracked window. Beyond the filthy glass panes, I glimpse two dark shapes shrinking as they fly toward the Heart.

"Surveillance drones," Ezra grunts under his breath.

Ezra and Jenner don't question me further, and the room descends into uneasy silence, all of us avoiding eye contact as we each fall prey to our own troubled thoughts.

I may not fully remember what we went through together, but I've glimpsed enough, I *feel* enough of who I was, to want to keep them both safe. The trouble is, I don't know how to do that. Up until now, I only ever used this power to destroy. The one and only time I considered protecting anyone with it was when the transport helicopter was seconds from crashing. In the end, I didn't bother. Rather than attempt to save those soldiers, I caved to my impulses and selfish desire for freedom and let them all die so that I could die, too.

A startling realization occurs to me. What if I'm incapable of using my condition for good? What if, by trying to protect one, I inadvertently cause harm to the other? Could I live with that?

Could I live with being responsible for the death of yet another person I love?

AUSTIN B. RICHTER

AGE: 25-28

BLOOD TYPE: A+

HEIGHT: 6'2

HAIR COLOR: AUBURN

EYE COLOR: GRAY

Dr.
AUSTIN RICHTER
Dr.
AUSTIN RICHTER

"True or false. You love me." I bite my lower lip, hating how timid I sound. How starved for some assurance of his affection.

Cupping my face in his hands again, he pulls me in for another kiss. He starts at my forehead, then kisses me once on each cheek, before ending at my lips.

"True," he whispers into my mouth.

Our movements become frantic after that. My fingers work to remove his soaked clothes, while his hands explore my body and tangle in my hair, tugging my head back for better access to my throat. His teeth skim my collarbone as his voice hums against my skin and three beautiful words rise up to my ear in his low, haunting timbre.

"I missed you."

We pause for a moment just to stare at each other. Then, not wanting to waste another second on words, we lose ourselves under the water.

A malicious grin disfigures his face. "But you wouldn't wish that on an innocent, would you? You're not willing to let *everyone* die, to watch the people you *love* die…are you?"

He pauses beside a white wall-like partition positioned on the right side of the room. I watch his hand with building unease as it swipes across the control panel beside it, the embedded screen jolting to life at the touch of his long, slender fingers.

"You're not willing to let *her* die…"

He presses a button on the computerized panel, and the solid barriers turn transparent, revealing a hospital bed surrounded on three sides by life support machines. An unconscious woman with warm brunette hair and light brown skin lies on top of the blankets like a specimen ready for dissection. Although she doesn't move, the monitor beside her head displays every beat of her heart, each upward tick on the screen coinciding with a shrill beep that I failed to hear before now. Each strike slashes through me like a knife to the chest.

My hands fly to my mouth as her name escapes me.

A second gunshot cracks through the buzzing in my ears and skull, and then the guard behind Jenner jerks back and collapses. His top-heavy frame collides hard with the ground.

I glance between the two guards, only looking at each of them long enough to confirm they're dead. Blood pools beneath their unmoving bodies, seeping over the weeds and staining the earth a deep crimson so dark the dirt appears black.

I redirect my gaze over my shoulder, a smile working its way onto my lips. Ezra and Jenner each turn as well, gaping at Quinn in disbelief.

The ex-Enforcer doesn't return our questioning stares or offer any explanation for his actions—he just scowls at us as he always does and fires one final shot in the air.

Three shots. One for each of us…should anyone be counting.

QUINN C. STOHLER

AGE: 20

BLOOD TYPE: A-

HEIGHT: 5'11

HAIR COLOR: BRUNETTE

EYE COLOR: BLACK

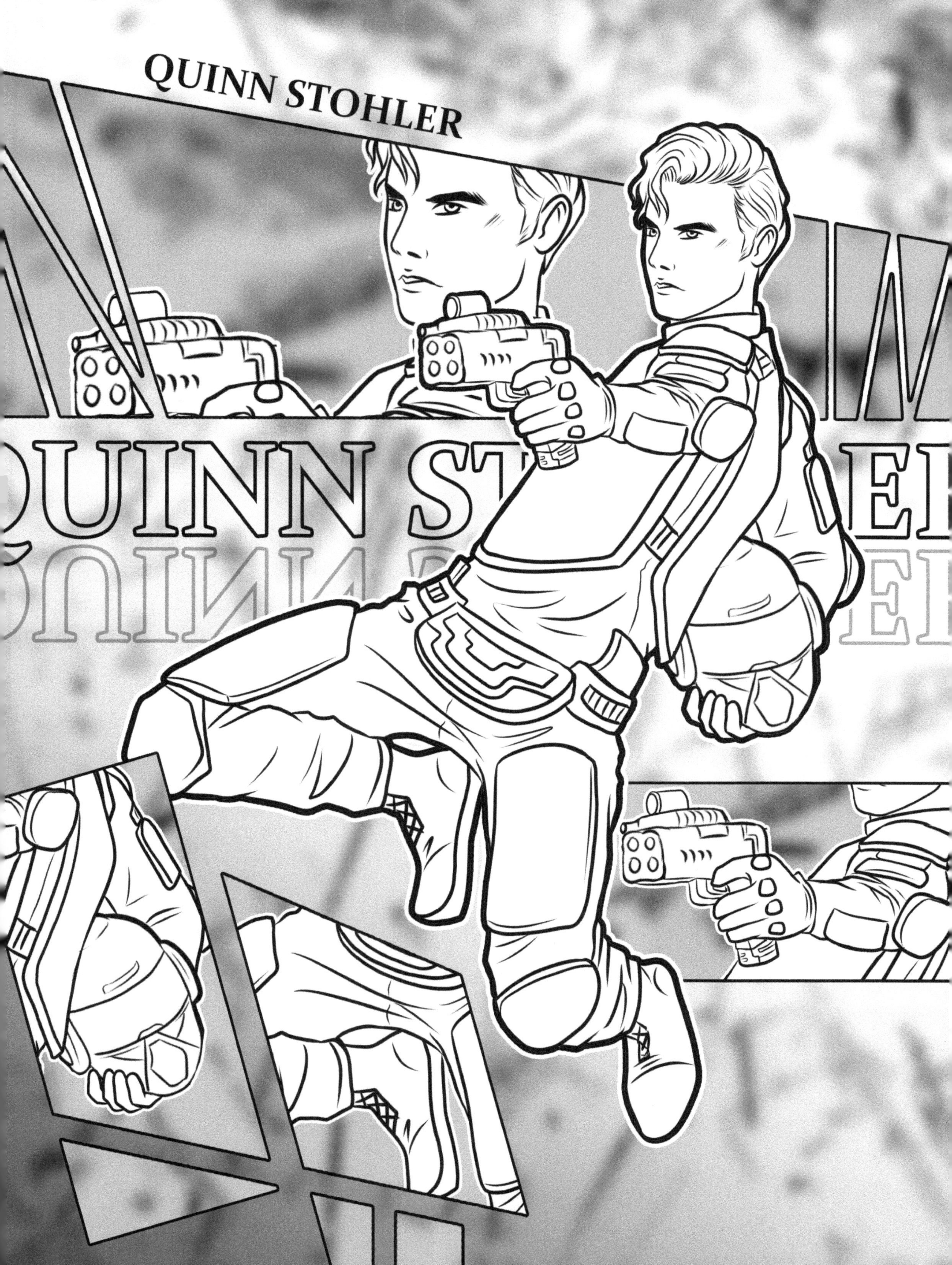
QUINN STOHLER

Fear prickles my skin as I lock onto Jenner and Quinn where they crouch behind a smoking abandoned car twenty or so feet away. The stretch of space between us seems to grow over the seconds we wait.

Ezra crushes me close to his chest, his racing heart thumping against my back, matching every frantic beat of my pulse. His grip on me tightens when beams of light flash across the ground just beside our hiding place, shining off a scattered nest of broken glass in which I catch glimpses of my distorted reflection. Although the light shifts away a few seconds later, I hold my breath, recognizing the vibrating sound of tires treading over debris. Each *crack* and *pop* gives me flashbacks to the trucks I was always transported in to my missions.

When the vehicle's engine cuts out, I lick my lips and peek around the edge of the wall. Less than fifty feet away, an armored truck stands vacant in the middle of the road, surrounded by at least ten Enforcers, who descend from the back one at a time, like an assembly line of death. The clomp of their boots against the pavement is deafening.

"You know," he whispers in my ear, "I spent the last two years trying to create more of you at the urging of my superiors, but every single time, the experiment failed. No matter what I tried, none of the others could come close to matching your genetic perfection. You are one of a kind, just like the beautiful poison blood that runs through your veins, and it was always meant to be you and me. We were meant to come together and see this through to the end. And now that you're with me again, we can. We can finish this, just as my mother predicted."

That terrible smile—the one that always contorted his face when he tortured me—spreads over his face again now, and he laughs a truly mad laugh, clutching me tightly by the back of my head and pulling me close until our noses are touching.

"What you fail to understand is that I don't wish to save this world. I wish to see it *burn*. Now that I have Raina again, my greatest desire is to witness the denouement of your vision. To see how this planet will come to its end."

BLOOD **DEMANDS** BLOOD.

SUBJECT ZERO

A smirk hooks up one edge of his lips. "I'm already awake."

Ezra thrusts his arms upward, slamming a large, flat object into the side of Richter's skull with such force that, for a moment, I allow myself the gleeful belief that my tormentor might be dead. The collision makes a tinny, metallic sound that results in a wobbling echo.

On impact, Richter's head snaps to the left, his glasses knocked to the floor, the frames bent and broken, the lenses cracked. For a few seconds, he teeters on his feet before crumpling, his gray eyes rolling back in their sockets.

Exhaling, Ezra drops his weapon, the medical tray clanging loudly against the white tiles. His chest heaves as he lets out a breath, and after checking with a nudge of his foot that Richter is unconscious, he finally looks in my direction.

"Thank you for bringing Wynter to me. You've upheld your end of the deal and I will see to it that I uphold mine."

Deal?

Acid sloshes against the walls of my stomach and my heart drops into my feet when I turn, following her line of sight to the unapologetic sable eyes watching me.

A breath catches in my throat. Was this what Quinn meant when he said he was saving my life? By making a deal to return me to my mother? But how would they even know one another?

He says nothing as I stare at him, his face increasingly pale, his breathing ragged. Any sympathy I felt for being the reason he got shot has evaporated like water in dry heat. Of course, he never really wanted to help us. He never cared about us finding Rai or preventing the war against the Heart that he helped to ignite by being Nolan's lackey and keeping me out of the State's hands. By keeping me captive. The whole time he's been playing both sides. The whole time he's been playing *me*, moving me around like a chess piece across a board I wasn't even aware I was on.

RODRICK A. NOLAN

AGE: 58

BLOOD TYPE: B+

HEIGHT: 6'1

HAIR COLOR: ASH BLOND

EYE COLOR: BLUE

RODRICK NOLAN

"My blood did this," I breathe, my voice cracking. "I did this."

Ezra sweeps my sweaty hair back from my forehead and wipes the blood off my quivering lips with the sleeve of his shirt.

"No, you didn't," he says fervently. "You were just…"

The pawn. The murder weapon.

Fresh tears slide down my cheeks, singeing my skin with their heat, as Ezra pulls me against his chest, hooking his chin over the top of my head. "I know it's hard to see otherwise, to *believe* otherwise, but none of this is your fault," he whispers.

I want to believe that, but how can I?

After everything he's seen me do, how can he?

My gaze drifts up to the observation deck window where I envision Dr. Richter just on the other side of that glass. I never wanted this. I never chose to become this tool, this weapon.

I hear footsteps behind me, then a familiar hand touches my shoulder before moving to my wrist, steadying my grip.

"Together," Ezra murmurs.

Guiding the needle, he presses my shaking thumb down on the plunger, then takes me into his arms as we watch the silver liquid travel through the length of the tube.

It takes less than ten seconds for the poison to enter Rai's body. When it reaches her heart, the monitor tracking her vitals beeps erratically, screaming in protest like the alarm we heard earlier. Unlike the alarm, it dies quickly, settling into one continuous tone.

As the tears roll fat and hot down my cheeks, the flatline rings around us like a death knell.

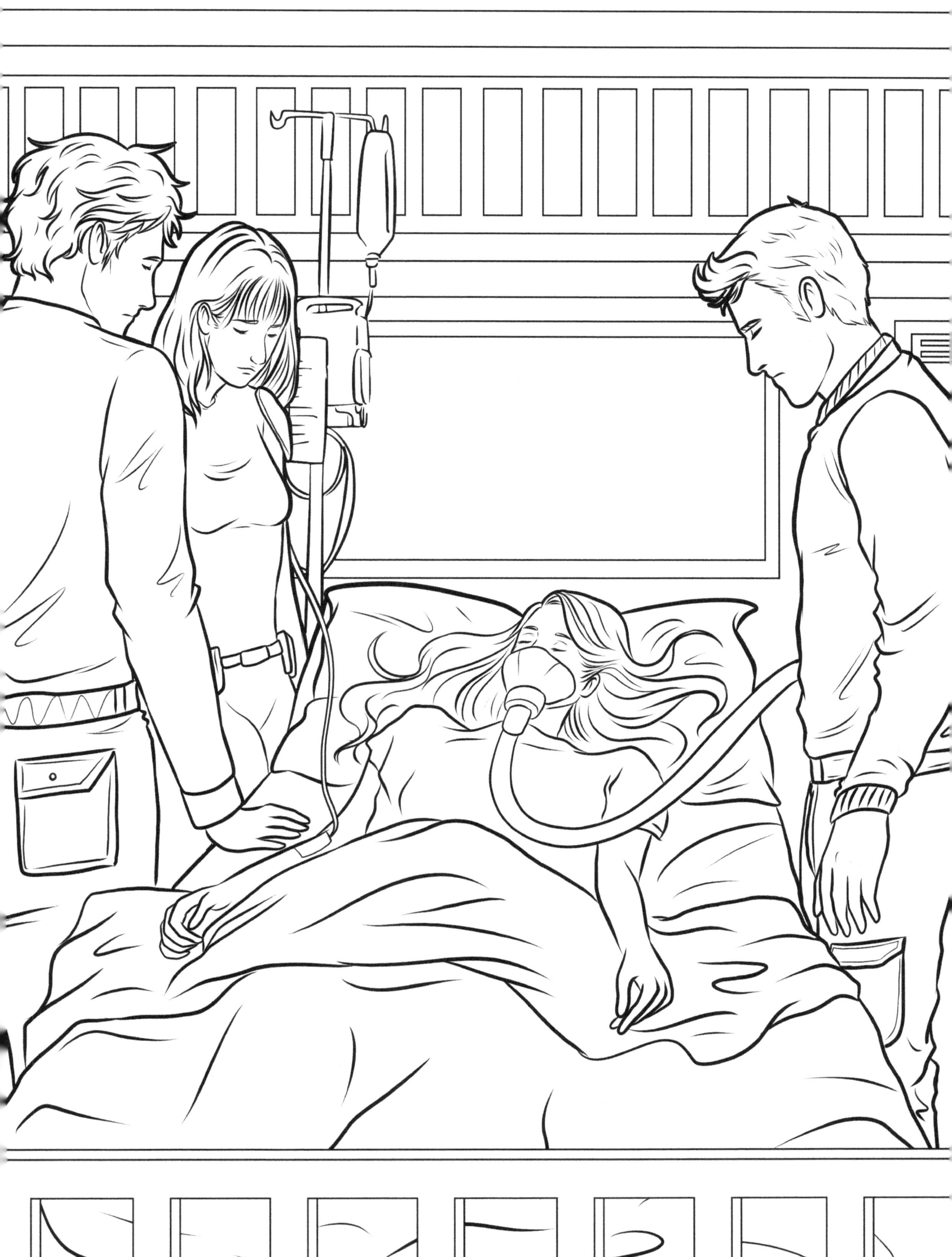

Beside me, Ezra stiffens. "I've been wondering, what would the Head of Termination need a safe house for?"

The unease and doubt in his voice set me on edge, and I glare at my mother as all the many reasons I had not to trust her pop into my head again.

Her lips curl almost imperceptibly at the corners. "It's not mine," she clarifies.

My blood runs cold at the scuffle of footsteps behind me, and wheeling around, I choke back the murderous instincts of my power as I come face to face with our true host.

Wren Bilken meets my gaze with a glower. "Hello again, Miss Reeves."

WREN O. BILKEN

AGE: 53

BLOOD TYPE: O+

HEIGHT: 6'2

HAIR COLOR: BLACK

EYE COLOR: BROWN

WREN BILKEN
WREN
KEN

Lacing my fingers through his disheveled hair, I snake my other arm around him and tug him down until our bodies are flush. As I hold him to me, stroking his back and head, he shakes with silent sobs.

"Please," I whisper again, pleading.

He swallows loudly. Then, nodding against my shoulder, he gives me the only thing I'm asking him for.

"I promise," he says, his voice husky.

My lips find his in the pained hush that follows, but as our fingers interlace, our bodies joining, a flicker of doubt seeps into the cracks in my thoughts. And as that doubt festers, I can't help wondering if, like so many other aspects of my life…

If those words are just another lie.

I step forward, drawing in a steadying breath, and as my feet reach the edge of the truck bed, Quinn's gaze shoots up from the cracked pavement, locking on mine. Inhaling again, I close my eyes.

The power in my mind is like tentacles reaching out, searching for the soldiers' heartbeats and using the draw of each *thump* to pinpoint their positions around us. I sense six in total.

This time, instead of expanding outward, the bubble of pressure in my chest is like a black hole, ready to suck everything in.

To destroy.

I call that destructive force to the surface before the soldiers are even aware of my presence, envisioning the bone structure of their spinal columns as I jerk my own head to the side. The sole Enforcer in my range of vision drops to the ground. To the side of the truck, I note the identical thud of a limp body hitting dirt.

"Wynter, stop!" someone shouts, grabbing my arm, but I throw them off, refusing to let them stand in my way. They crash to the floor with a grunt, and as I turn to face them, I take in the result of my wrath. Bodies everywhere—some soldiers, most not. Few, if any, are left standing.

I turn, concentrating on the figure bold enough to attack me, ready to eviscerate him like I did the others, when I glimpse the pitiful gun in his hand and the hazel eyes staring at me, pleading for the monster to stop. The pistol shakes in the man's grip, but he doesn't lower the barrel or point it away. His finger hovers over the trigger.

A tear cuts down his cheek. "Please," he begs, and I can see in the furrowed lines of his brow that he doesn't want to do this. He doesn't *want* to shoot me.

But he will.

He'll kill me to put an end to my rampage.

He'll kill me even though he loves me.

EVELYN P. ADLER

AGE: 51

BLOOD TYPE: O-

HEIGHT: 5'9

HAIR COLOR: BLONDE

EYE COLOR: BLUE

Dr. EVELYN ADLER

"All I've wanted the last two years and five months," he begins, his voice thready, "was for us to be together again. This way…we can."

He looks down at our hands, nudging my chest with his palm, and as he pulls me close, my mind reels back over every time he uttered that word.

"Together…" I echo. How many times have we said this? How many times have we sworn it to each other—sworn not to leave the other behind?

A vow that outweighs the promise he's broken.

His hand combs through my hair, brushing the sweaty strands away from my face, and as I stare at him, taking in his features for the last time, I realize his tears have stopped. His expression is resolved, the love in his hazel eyes undeterred.

"Always," he swears.

"We take it one day at a time and do whatever we can to create a world they would be proud of."

Quinn cocks a dubious eyebrow, crossing his arms. "Just like that, huh?" he asks skeptically.

Drawing in a trembling breath, I turn my gaze to the Heart, which, although fractured, will heal with time. The last of the diminishing daylight glows around it like a halo, giving me hope.

And before it all, in the distance, I swear I see Wynter. She looks at me with that shy smile I loved from the first time I saw it and has one hand outstretched, urging me forward.

As I take a step, lured by her beckoning, I recite the words I carved into her tombstone, and through my pain, they give me courage. The courage to keep fighting for the future she gave herself to protect.

SHE SAVED US ALL

"Yup." A smile tugs at one corner of my lips. "Just like that."

Wynter Reeves
SHE SAVED US ALL.
Ezra Laramie
A FRIEND.
A BROTHER

IF YOU COULD SEE THE FUTURE...

HOW FAR WOULD YOU GO

TO CHANGE IT?

PROJECT
W. A. R.